LAST VANITIES

FLEUR JAEGGY

LAST VANITIES

TRANSLATED BY TIM PARKS

A NEW DIRECTIONS BOOK

Published by arrangement with Adelphi Edizioni, Milan. Originally published in 1994
as *La paura del cielo*.

Design by Sylvia Frezzolini Severance
First published as a New Directions Paperbook Original in 1998.
Manufactured in the United States of America.
New Directions Books are printed on acid-free paper.
Published simultaneously in Canada by Penguin Books Canada Limited.

Library of Congress Cataloging-in Publication Data:

Jaeggy, Fleur.
    [Paura del cielo.   English]
    Last vanities / Fleur Jaeggy ; translated by Tim Parks.
       p.   cm.
    ISBN 0-8112-1374-9 (alk. paper)
    I. Parks, Tim.   II. Title.
    PQ4870.A4P3813   1998
    853'.914—dc21   97-44496
                                                     CIP

New Directions Books are published for James Laughlin
by New Directions Publishing Corporation
80 Eighth Avenue, New York 10011

CONTENTS

LAST VANITIES

NO DESTINY

NO DESTINY

Then she hated her. Marie Anne had spent all afternoon pruning, more than was necessary. She gave herself up to her rage. Cleaning mainly. The soil was soft, it had rained. And looked dirty. Her garden was in a courtyard, the sun couldn't get at the earth. Uncertain, the heat stopped at the outside wall. A small thing, that garden. Damp. White in winter. Dirty white. In spring it was dirtier still, the cold and decay wouldn't leave that patch of soil alone. In summer it was dry. And the years were slipping by. Marie Anne sits in the garden pushing the pram against the wall with her foot. Then pulling it back with a piece of string. So the baby could move about a bit. The little girl looked dumbly around. Marie Anne had hated her from the moment she appeared in the world. She appeared along with a hundred other newborns, there was a tag, and that was her daughter. Normal. She wasn't blind, her hearing was good. Her friend Johanna wanted to have the child. She was a half-caste. "If you don't like her, why not give her to me?" Johanna had gone on and on. And even the people she worked for—Johanna was a maid—would have liked to have the girl. If you don't like her, let us look after her. We'll adopt her. Marie Anne had seen the nice house Johanna's employers had. And the nice garden. The white wicker chairs, so elegant and uncomfortable. They showed her the girl's room too. A little bed that looked like cream and strawberry ice. In another room there were toys. The toys of Johanna's employers' little girl that died. No one had touched them since. Sometimes, in the evening, the mother rocked the rocking horse. You can't play with a dead child's toys. That's what her husband said. A sensible fellow, he would have liked to play with his dead daughter's dolls himself. The dolls laughed at this man and woman who couldn't forget their baby. They were still intact. The little girl hadn't had time to smash in their faces or pull off their legs or maybe an arm. It saddened the wife: this lack of wear and tear precluding renewal. Premature toys. Even the dolls' clothes were intact. Ironed. Their hair too. Lots of soft little wigs in their boxes. Blond, black, with curls even, like Johanna's. Their daughter never combed them. But perhaps she's doing it now. In her cute little grave she combs and combs their hair, like Lorelei. The wife wonders about that. But the husband said it was impossible and that she mustn't think of such things. That deep down he thinks of himself.

His daughter was growing in her grave. She would have been five now. And it made no difference that it was a heap of dust doing the playing. They wouldn't have any other children. And they felt extremely pleased now to be showing their daughter's room to Marie Anne. Marie Anne looked everything over with stubborn amazement. She felt generous praising it all, she thought it would please the woman that someone was saying she had done up her dead daughter's room so well. The wallpaper was red cherries and white irises with leaves. There was even a little table with a mirror for the child. Where she would look at herself while Johanna braided her hair. Everything arranged as if she were already a little woman. The child's clothes were still in the closet. All pink. The little shoes at the bottom. Ready to run. Some of them white. Some in blue calfskin. On the top shelf were some little straw hats. It was summertime. Johanna was so hot she couldn't work. In the evening, before going to bed, she would sit by the window with her legs spread wide. Even the lawn was sweating. Voices came from far away. Even they sounded sweaty. No color to the sky. When it's very hot, it gets like an infected sheet, and she saw bad luck in that sheet. But then she went to sleep almost at once, a heavy sleep. She didn't like her life that much. Marie Anne said that was because she didn't like men. What Johanna liked was bending down for hours and hours wiping the floor. Then going to sleep. She was still good-looking. There was nothing she really liked. Unless maybe the people she worked for. Because they were sad. They hid it. When she served them at table they pretended to be happy. You don't have to laugh to pretend you're not sad, she thought. They were never vulgar. Their laughter is instructive. When Johanna laughs she's vulgar. She laughed for joy when Marie Anne's baby was born. Everybody in the hospital heard her. But Johanna wasn't Marie Anne's husband. Even though they'd once been to bed together. Johanna couldn't give Marie Anne a baby. Perhaps everything had happened after Marie Anne had been to bed with Johanna. Towards dawn she went out for a walk. And nine months later Johanna had laughed at the hospital. Nine months had passed. In her head she thought of herself as the father. When Marie Anne said: "I don't want her, take her away," the baby had been in her arms, where a nurse had put her. Then Johanna had begun to think of being both mother and father to the girl. "Give her to me, give me the baby," she had asked, over and over. And now her employers kept asking too. Johanna knew her employers would win. The child would grow up rich and respectable. She would be her maid, as she had been the dead child's. Marie Anne looked round and found she liked the room. "It would be just fine for my baby," she said, "that's for sure." And at the same time she was thinking of the room where her daughter slept now, a narrow room with no windows. But if you left the door open it did get a little grey light from the kitchen window. Johanna had given her the crib, the little undershirts, and all the rest. Johanna went into the shops and asked for clothes for her daughter: "I had a little girl a few days ago," she told them. The assistants congratulated her. She only bought the best and went proudly back to

Marie Anne's, where the mother spent all day in the garden, pruning—and cursing.

Hearing those curses, Johanna feared what the heavens might do. She held the baby tight. To hide her from the heavens. Johanna's employers kept inviting Marie Anne to visit. They invited her to lunch. Marie Anne behaved like a lady almost. She watched how the wife served herself and then did the same. She smiled sweetly at the woman's husband. She said a few things about herself, concealing the worst. Johanna had even given her some evening clothes. Black dresses, stylish. One day the woman's husband gave her a pearl necklace. Another day the wife gave her a gold bracelet with a diamond. All things that would have belonged to the little girl who had died. But now they must grace the mother of a child who was alive and might become their child. For it looked as though Marie Anne would give up her daughter. Who lay in her pram in the garden, pushed with a kick and jerked back with a string. The child could hardly have imagined what a splendid future was to be hers. Her mild eyes turned, it seemed, to the void, in an unbearable way. It was still too soon. One supposes. At that age you don't think about your destiny.

More months went by. Marie Anne wore more and more jewelry. Johanna doesn't say: "Give your little girl to me," anymore. By now the little girl has been promised to her employers. She watches her employers embrace Marie Anne. They had tears in their eyes. They went into the toy room and crouching down all three of them began to play. Marie Anne got on the woman's husband's back and the woman laughed holding a doll in her hand. Like a battle-ax. Johanna brought them drinks. They celebrated. They put wigs on their glasses. That night the dolls were no longer a cult of the dead, but dolls to disembowel, pull to bits with pleasure. They dressed and undressed them, even the wife took off her dress. They played at being happy. Happiness bit into them like a burning blade. They shook hands to settle the deal. Marie Anne gave a look of triumph. She gave her word of honor. She laid it down before them. It was a spring day and getting late. Marie Anne wasn't in the habit of speaking a great deal, dragging things out that is. To her mind the origin of speech, and creation, was the curse. Now Marie Anne had promised. "My daughter will be yours."

The wooden horse was still rocking at dawn. Johanna claimed it rocked for days. While the dolls sat still and gazed.

At home, Marie Anne went to her child. She was asleep. She watched her for a long time. Next morning she took her into the muddy garden. Marie Anne couldn't find anything else to prune. She held the pruning shears in her hands. And didn't know who to use them on. She looked at her child. She won't have a nice destiny. I won't leave her to those people. She won't have a nice house. Why should that little girl she hated have a better life? She wrote a letter to Johanna's employers. "I've changed my mind. It was a joke." Goodbye. The wife hung herself five minutes later. Like the rocking horse, her body swung back and forth. The child has grown up. Marie Anne hates her. Yesterday they walked by the couple's big house and she told the girl every-thing. She had been promised to that house. The girl is fif-teen now and she often walks by that house. People say she's a little dumb. But she's not. She's just looking at her destiny. Or rather, at where destiny passed her by.

1

A WIFE

A WIFE

It was a good marriage. The Rueggs lived in the country, ran a livestock farm. The wife, Gretel, was a prudent woman. Perhaps as a girl, before marrying, she'd occasionally been curious about the world, but this faded soon enough. The years went by and all her curiosity with them. First there were the cows, then three daughters. Every two years. Right on time. At thirty-five Gretel was a proud mother. She helped the cows give birth, had given birth herself. But while the animals seemed indifferent to their fate, Gretel was afraid of hers. A shadow had fallen over her, was tormenting her. Her happiness was marred. On seeing the baby girls in their cribs her husband had covered his face with his big strong hands. "It's a curse," he'd yelled. "It's a curse," he yelled when the third arrived. Everyone heard those shouts, the boys at their work, the cows, the country-side. As if the bleak wind that whips the dry shrubs into wreaths had carried the railing voice far away, as far as the border with Czechoslovakia. It was the voice of Otto Karl Ruegg.

The landscape didn't answer his shouts, the voice drifted about the plain, then fell silent. The cows twitched their ears, pained by the shouts. An old maid, who had served Otto's father before him, smiled, not with her mouth, but with her eyes. A strange gleam kindled her withered skin, conferring an unsuspected ardor.

She always addressed Otto's wife as "gnädige Frau." From day one she'd disliked her. She'd been dressed in white, a pretentious, overdressed peasant, with creamy cheeks, flowers and barrettes in her hair. Her train slid across freshly manured earth. The Rueggs danced. The farmboys danced and she, the faithful servant, sat on a wooden bench. She was wearing a dress Otto's mother had given her that came down to her ankles. She kept her feet together in black lace-up shoes. Her arms folded. Her arms tightly folded.

Come the evening she helped her new mistress undress. The wedding bedroom was full of flowers, smelled sickening. From the window you could see the cattle pen and the fields. The old servant picked up the wedding dress and took it away, pressing that pointless, tainted lace to her breast.

She could call her Gretel, her mistress said. And, if the older woman agreed, she would use her first name too. She rubbed her hands, in raptures over her wedding. She was so lucky. Gretel wanted to hug the old servant. She stood there with her hands together, perhaps the servant didn't dare call her by name, but Gretel begged her, timorous and happy. Otto had said so much about her. The old woman watched unmoved. She had obeyed orders in the family, the orders of the previous generation, but she had not shared their happiness. One didn't make a great fuss over fortune and happiness, in those days. One was obliged to rejoice when one's masters had reason to, it was part of one's general obedience, and sometimes she had rejoiced. When Otto Karl was born, the first and the last of the children. She had rejoiced over the first and the last. The mother died in childbirth. And the old woman became the ghostly shade of her dead mistress. If the dead leave unsatisfied desires, their shades can claim them for themselves. It was she who went to choose the best breasts in the country to nurse young Otto Karl.

The newlyweds set off on their honeymoon. The old woman took all the flowers from the room, put them on a cart, and drove them to the cemetery. "These are the flowers your son's wife was given, do with them as you see fit."

Aside from rotting, there's little flowers can do, and in this they are not unlike human beings. Flowers and corpses are in a race to turn to forgotten dust, thought the old woman. The dead know what to do with the flowers left on their stones. They know how to repay those who gave them. They know how to avenge a gift. If they don't like it. They might like a pointless prayer. Or a change of heart. Nothing is so potent as the empty gesture.

Standing by the stone the servant held her thoughts with thick bridles and felt as though she were riding away. She rode to Bohemia, where her ancestors lay, a hunting dog and her wet nurse. And the wind. Long frozen winters and the fatal geometry of winter whiteness. Lines loomed vertically like abandoned crosses, then bent all together at the first shift in the wind. Wind can bend crosses. There were storms, mud and marshes, a heavy, sulfurous breeze casting a spell over those who had lost their way.

Then the servant sat down on the gravestone and described the bride. She praised her beauty and the way she stood and moved. She praised her hips and waist. The quality of her hair and teeth. She closed her eyes. Her hands unraveled what features of Gretel's were still imprinted on the back of her eyes. Her gestures were quick as a deaf-mute's. Finally she laid the image she had evoked down on the stone. Clouds darkened the sky and a passerby might have thought that someone had forgotten to take away a figure of clay. She said goodbye to her mistress, a woman she had scarcely known. She'd been so young, had only stopped by the house to leave a baby there, asked nothing more. They hadn't been married long, she hadn't flaunted that acme of exultancy, the disease happiness is. Meekly she spread out her hopes. And the servant spread the sheet.

The Rueggs' honeymoon lasted only a few days. Otto Karl was restless, would happily have gone home after the first night. With one's wife in one's bed, lovemaking seemed a sign of laziness. His wife was asleep now and his hand lay on the neck he had bitten only shortly before. He made plans. He wanted a slaughterhouse.

The following morning their breakfast was brought to them in bed. It was a generous petit déjeuner with cheeses, scrambled eggs, sausages, and cake. The price was included, the honeymoon package deal. And if there wasn't enough they could ask for more, as much as they wanted, without paying any extra. And this was to go on for seven days. Eating as much as they wanted. The days allotted to the newlyweds. He explained the advantages of a slaughterhouse. He could afford it. It was for the future. For their children. For the children conceived in one of those hotel rooms where honeymooning couples go with nothing else to do. Their food keeping fresh in the big refrigerators of hotel kitchens. German couples, most of them. Every evening a different menu, exotic even, accompanied by the authentic music of the places the food came from. The Mexican night. If you wanted you could wear a sombrero. Or the Shanghai night. Or Spain. Italienische Nacht. The German couples enjoyed these distractions, having taken possession of each other's bodies.

On their way home the Rueggs spent a further night in Munich, at the Vierjahreszeiten. They went to bed. Husband kissed wife. Rather than passion it was a heavy, dull pressure. Before going to sleep he called her "my wife, my housewife." She felt all the primordial intensity of the words, an investiture that cloaked her whole body and filled the dark room, the curtains on the windows that seemed to be made of zinc. She would have liked to conceive at that very moment. As, already half-asleep, Ruegg pronounced the word: "housewife."

The faithful old servant was waiting for them at the front door. From far away she looked like an urn, small, gloomy, dignified. Every morning Gretel got up at half past five. But the servant was already in the kitchen, had already set the table for everyone. "Up so early, gnädige Frau?" she would say. "Why don't you sleep? You need to." Gretel wasn't looking after herself now, she wore big smocks, heavy shoes, socks rolled down to her ankles. She had an anxious look about her. A look that keeps watch over the progress of the house. The inner progress. Of the perfect house. She has to think of the morality of the farmhands too. And when she sees them laugh she gets worried. Because if they're laughing in that sly way it can only be about sex. Only sex can make those boys laugh, with that sharp, cagey look they have. If they're interested in something it's because of sex. She was sure of that.

And her daughters had begun to whisper among themselves and she had to keep an eye on them. The old servant, who never missed a thing, told her gnädige Frau not to worry. It was nature. They had fistfights with the farmboys. Otto Karl watched and said: "Look how your daughters can fight." And those sturdy girls fought hard. Even when they were small they went at it, twisting their legs round the boys' backs. Gretel got the water pump and soaked them, in a frenzy, as if watering a parched forest.

Gretel got migraines. While her daughters were growing. She checked the sofa in the sitting room, the cushions had to be hard. Apprehensively, she surveyed the country-side, the meadows, the barns, the trucks, anywhere her daughters could lie down. Sundays they were free to stay out all day. Sometimes they came home late. She waits up for them. Studies their faces. The girls have shiny eyes, misty eyes, and smell of beer. She went into their room at night, and watched them sleep. What were they doing with their bodies, when they pretended to fight with the farmhands? The old servant kept telling the gnädige Frau to relax, she should sleep at night, she shouldn't get herself in a state. Nature follows its course, its inclinations. Torpor in the room, the paddock is empty, the house is quiet. The house is ruled by instincts. By instincts and nothing else. That's what Gretel said.

One evening, after dinner, they had all drunk a lot of beer. For once even Gretel was making jokes and innuendos. She had taken off her smock and her tight dress still betrayed the curves of a fine heifer. So said Otto Karl. Pushing her, making her twirl. Then Gretel got into the swing, was spinning on her own. The boys drummed their knuckles on the table. Gretel stamped her feet to their rhythm. Dropping her head she surged forward. She felt light, it seemed all those bodies around her were emptied of passion and sin. The master of the house was having fun, he'd never seen her so merry, he saw a heifer in her, about to be sacrificed. He lifted his beer mug and made a toast: "Auf den Tod." The wife repeated as though she were an echo: "Auf den Tod." "To death," and downed her beer. The boys drummed their knuckles on the table. Inspired, she spun in her circle.

The boys were young, they loved the beasts they killed. They didn't want them to suffer. They started the job before they were thirteen. Their hands tell far more than their faces or glazed eyes. The brain lags behind the hands. There's a strange nostalgia in their heads, something unreal, frivolous, enchanting. It was Otto took them on, children but already adults, he liked their serious eyes, that haze they still had in their heads, that slowness, that heavy slowness that never caught up with the deftness of their hands. He liked their frowns when he gave orders or explained something. Callow men they were, some with shaved heads. The youth of those meek, stubborn skulls. They were like brothers to the cattle. Otto Karl had the greatest respect for brotherhood and gave it the utmost importance. Knuckles drum on the table. Have been drumming for years it seems. Ever since he saw those baby girls in their cradles. His mind wanders in an intoxicating gloom. That obsessive, goading, brotherly rhythm, as if it were a single voice, a single thought, like a sickening drumroll.

"To the devil," his wife thought. And the devil she would have liked to dance with was one of the freshly slaughtered calves seated on a golden throne, with earrings. She was licking its hoofs as a sign of devotion. After the fatal blow the animals ascend to heaven, while she was merry and felt she was still a good-looking heifer. Her husband had just said as much, in front of the boys, that she was a good-looking heifer. And so be it. He hadn't humiliated her. It was something animal in her dancing, she could feel the animal squeezing her like a corset. It was fury and annihilation that was beating the time, panting out the rhythm, keeping pace with the stealthy tread of catastrophe. She was adoring her kind, who before becoming butcher's meat had been happy, contemplative, wise. Nervous sometimes. Submissive. She had stroked them. She had stroked everything that oozed from their impassive muzzles. They had already, she dared to think, suffered the mortal blow.

The farmboys look like inlay carved in the wooden wall. Bavarian novices, sentimental and barbaric. A drunken torpor has them in its thrall, closing up their faces. The curves of their eyelids. Gretel would like to sacrifice one. With their right hands they raise their beer mugs. It's party time. She would like to show her husband she knows how to kill. As well as the best of them. People shouldn't curse women who only have girls. Just because they can't do their father's jobs when they grow up. Her girls have no passion for the slaughterhouse. They've left home. Dorothea, the eldest, has changed her name. She has a Jewish name now. She is no longer Fräulein Ruegg. She's gone to live in Tuscany. The other, Roseli, lives in Berlin with a stripper. And the third hasn't stayed in touch. It's true, the slaughterhouse will have no heirs. Gretel feels lonely, she'd like to have grandchildren. There is nothing better than procreation. She and the animals know that. How pretty her daughters were in their cradles. The slightly oversize heads, the wispy hair, red blotches on their skin. The linen dangled from the spindle, she had embroidered their initials. Initials waiting to be ruined names.

She wishes everyone goodnight. Gloom for her husband who looks at her complacently from mongol eyes. The boys get to their feet. On the wooden staircase her steps go unheard. It's winter. The snow covers the countryside, leveling the earth in a drowsy panic. Perhaps only the ultimate truths can bring joy to Frau Ruegg, the farmer's wife. Like the winter landscape, dragged into an angelic and antique peace, her thoughts are buried in the frost. Thoughts free of words. Sacred inertia.

*   *   *

The writer was in Zurich reading the *Neue Zürcher Zeitung*. The funeral of an eminent butcher was to be held at three o'clock of a November afternoon. In the "Deaths" section it said that destiny had suddenly and inexplicably dealt the family a bitter blow. The word *jäh*, which means suddenly, stood out in its simplicity beside the word destiny. A brief sound. Irrevocable. Typographically elegant upon the page. The writer had written a story about a butcher and his wife. But he wasn't convinced by the ending. He thought: Perhaps I should go to a butcher's funeral. His hotel on the Limmat wasn't far from the Fraumunster. His room looked out over the river. At night he watched the swans sleeping on the water. The next day at a few minutes past three he was standing outside the church. The church was already packed. A woman was stopping people from going in. But you could climb up a narrow staircase to where the organ was. Here too it was already packed. Out of sheer impatience the service must have started early, at two minutes to three. Punctuality would be tardy. The pastor was delivering his sermon. A local accent, you could hear the dialect in his intonations. He'd told the story of the eminent butcher's life, his marriage, his career. His children. Looking toward the absent altar, you can see this is a first-class funeral. The pastor wonders whether the deceased's profession (killing animals) can be reconciled with the Christian way of life. The question is left unanswered. The pastor immediately changes the subject. The butcher's merits were many. Orphaned at eighteen, he set to work with great enthusiasm. With a sense of responsibility. He did everything possible to build up his business. Relatives and friends should not feel sad, pain brings its own relief. Pain is relief. From his pulpit in the exalted silence of the church the pastor exhorted everyone to find relief. To be appeased in their pain. The faces turned towards him were serious, contrite, a trifle absent. A trace of emptiness in their steady eyes. The composure of the void. They were so impassive it was as if they had bitten off their breath. The relatives sat in front of the congregation; together with the coffin they formed the altar. There weren't many flowers, as if some had faded already. The writer had found himself a place in a corner, near the heating pipes. He's trying to watch the people round him. They have dressed with care. In grey. Here and there a noble profile. A nervous stillness. A severe and heavy dignity. Were they all butchers? he wondered. A small group got up and began to sing. In a circle. Fine, mellow voices. "Our dreams they are no more." The pastor's voice sounds more distant, and likewise the words "pain" and "relief." They have lost their shape. Time too is standing still. The church is wrapped in the torpor of burnt-out thoughts. What struck one in those faces was a detachment at once profound and primitive, but not meek. Death does not move them. It is in the order of things. The savage secrecy of simple things. If they are so impassive, thought the intruder, the writer, still looking for an end to his story, perhaps it's because they abhor words and their variations. Those proud eyes were gazing at the essence. With their passionate reserve, they were gazing, so it seemed to him, at the invisible. When they heard a sound of hunting horns, their eyes sharpened. Cautious gleams. Quiet eyebrows lifted. In the bare Gothic church, its rage of depredation, purest stone, towards the sky, the sound of horns, so human, stirred a brief echo of exaltation in their minds.

*　　*　　*

The writer was still looking for an ending to his story. Endings should be portentous. Perhaps. The magnificent funeral might have helped. It didn't. You couldn't have Ruegg die because of the hunting horns. In her desperation, Gretel will find appeasement. Let's leave her watching the snow-covered landscape. In her sacred inertia. A last detail: the butcher's name was Angst, Fear.

THE FREE HOUSE

THE FREE HOUSE

Tenants are invited to remove perishable foods from the kitchen, open their doors or hand over their keys, for the exterminators. The notice is clearly visible in the entrance. It says: Products used to rid the building of roaches are not harmful to people or pets. The apartment building is not far from the lake. Lac Léman. There are four floors. It is painted pale pink. Across the street, an evangelical community center, bricks and barred windows. Around it a low wall and a hedge. Leaning on the wall, in the shadow, a black man. It's a damp, steamy day in April. The sun lingers, settles on the pink house. Everybody knows the woman who's passing by along the street. Even the man leaning on the wall doffs his cap. He doesn't go into the evangelical center, he likes to be outside. Every day, on a notice board near the gate, he finds the following words: "Eternal One, you plumb me and know me, you know when I sit and when I stand." Johnny keeps the notice board clean. He watches the people going by. He fills up bags, rummaging in the evangelicals' trash. Their consumption and waste are moderate. He has nothing else to do. He is another of those Mr. Heber protects. Another who has no civil rights. That doesn't mean that he isn't free, he can wander about day and night. Just that he is considered to have lost the faculty of acting according to reason. And this means that he is unable to discriminate, according to the authorities. He smiles at Mrs. Heber, who walks down the street almost every day. Mrs. Heber is able to discriminate, even though at first glance there doesn't seem to be much difference between the two of them. She is a worthy woman, sixtyish perhaps, well built, hair brushed back. She walks by with purse and string bag, the man knows that Mrs. Heber pretends to be doing the shopping. There are also Turkish workers, leaning against the wall.

"Good morning." "Getting a bit of sunshine, Johnny?" Johnny was leaning in the only shady place along the wall. "Why not take a walk by the lake? There's ice cream everywhere now." So colorful. Johnny doesn't like ice cream and Mrs. Heber knows perfectly well that he doesn't have any money. They give him what little he needs to eat, he tops it off with the trash he finds, and his room comes free. His room comes free, thanks to Mr. Heber. They are all there, in that street, in that four-story house, with its elevator. A little further down, towards the lake, there's a big hotel with obliquely set windows so that even those with a room on the side have a view of the lake. The evangelical community marks the boundary with an invisible line. After the church, the houses are middle-class, ornamented, pompous almost. Before the church, stucco peeling off the walls, other houses await the exterminators. The lake breeze wafts by, though the air is often stale. Prematurely stale, for the month of April. It's suffocating and Mrs. Heber has on a flowery, short-sleeved dress. The man, Monsieur Johnny, is never hot. He is wise, calm. He thanks heaven he is not dead or in prison, or trussed up in a straitjacket. He has ample time to die a second time. And he seems to be contemplating that moment. The being able to do so in peace, with free accommodation, handouts, and the evangelicals' trash. For this he is thankful to Mr. Heber. For having ample time to croak, day after day, as though telling a rosary, each year a copy of the year before. His one obligation: to see the social worker, a white woman with thin fine hair, pale, short-sighted eyes, and an expression of cautious reproach. As if Johnny's "thank you" were an outrage. And that glint in his eyes impertinence.

In the house provided for those, and only those, who have no civil rights, lives a Swiss man whose son was murdered. He says it was the social worker's fault. He toasts sweet almonds all day long. His wife refused to keep him. Now he is a mild man, filling small plastic bags with almonds and sticking on a label with his name. He has permission to sell them for two francs fifty. His room is very clean, the walls full of photographs. All of his son, from childhood on, up to the age when they killed him. And postcards of places. Places he went on vacation with his wife and son. Not many of those in the house have memories. Or not memories to flaunt. A photograph is proof. Some only have them in their heads. He is also the only one to have had a family, a real family. He was a pastry cook. He says it with pride. It's not a job he's invented for himself since they put him in this free accommodation. And deprived him of his civil rights. He comes, if one can use the term, from normality. He had a wife, une garce, he says, a slut who left him to go off with others. And a son, whom he lost. This is respectable. He sometimes naps during the day in his room, which has a sweet smell. He's the only one to have geraniums on the windowsill. Together with Johnny, he's the only one who keeps his windows open. On alternate days, there's another tenant who also keeps his windows open. His room is full of bottles and old clothes. Outside his door it says *Chopin*. With a few notes on a stave. In the evening he goes out with his hat, which has a feather, velvet trousers, and a stick. Mrs. Heber knows them all very well. They owe this to her husband. Their free life. Others, in other countries, are dying in the street. Here, they have all they need.

Ever since she and Mr. Heber married he has had a genuine passion for these creatures, but his wife put it down to youthful idealism. Or to his wanting to impress her, with his altruism, his thinking about humanity and the well-being of mankind. The first years of their marriage were not entirely without pleasant emotions. She liked being Mrs.

Heber, wife of a civil servant. Many owed their free food and board to him. They lived just a few yards from the middle classes, to whom she belonged. Every day her husband came home at the same time and she had his dinner waiting. Her husband was tired, but didn't let that stop him telling her the sad news. He got worked up. How often he spoke of the poor black. And the poor girl from the provincial asylum. Who turned prostitute. Because these women, he said, had no other salvation than the sale of their bodies. In the end, he said, they were free to do as they pleased. Those deprived of their civil rights can make what use they want of themselves. And the women, as soon as they were truly free to choose how to spend their time, this peaceful time they had, started seeing men. And in this regard, Mr. Heber was bound to be honest and confess, no one behaved as freely and open-mindedly as they. But this was hardly a crime, he went on to say. Though they shouldn't take advantage. On account of the house being free. One young girl had received as many as four or five men in her room in a single evening. Three were blacks, Americans. What Mr. Heber found strange, hard to understand, was the girl's extraordinary sexual appetite. He looked at his wife and waited for her to say something. His wife didn't know how to respond. She was embarrassed. Even after their marriage, and sleeping in the same bed with him, Mrs. Heber was still coy and Mr. Heber found that coyness slightly repugnant. "You are a good wife," he would tell her. And he began to stay out more. He came home late. Showed little inclination toward Mrs. Heber. In bed he turned his back to her and fell asleep. He had begun to snore too.

Mrs. Heber wasn't upset by her husband's lack of interest. Her sleep was unruffled. And during the day, when she had done the housework and the shopping, she would sit in the kitchen and daydream. She daydreamed. She dreamed of their life as a couple, right to the end. She was sure she would die first. Because do-gooding is easy, she thought. It makes you live longer. And she wondered who would look after him. She had written some memos for Mr. Heber. The receipts are in the drawer, likewise suppliers' names and phone numbers. Other times she dreamed that he went first. And then, since she felt a great deal of affection for this husband who no longer touched her at night, she would feel sad. And she wanted his body. He would stop helping these losers. That was her favorite dream. She prepared his funeral like a dinner. In the kitchen she expressed gratitude for condolences, talking to the carving knife. She took the knife and cut the roast. She poured out a glass of Dole.

She knew Johnny laughed at her, every time he saw her in the street outside the free house. The others too. She went there to spy. She wanted to see. She wanted to see the girl's sexuality. She wanted to see her. And she did. She was a young thing of about nineteen, the most recent arrival in the free house. Some months previously a tenant had died, a tenant who never bothered anyone. He shouted, then fell silent.

They disinfected his room, changed the wallpaper and the toilet fittings. Then the new tenant moved in to the room and bathroom. For her exclusive use. And for the first few weeks, it seems, she would lock herself in. She couldn't get used to the idea that no one was going to turn her out. Where she came from, the locks had been removed from the toilet doors. Now she lay on the floor in the bathroom, free to wash her hands over and over again. Mr. Heber had a cupboard installed. She pulled off the doors and smashed them, she was very strong. She put nails in the walls to hang her clothes on. Her clothes had to be visible. Having got over this early excitement about her accommodation, the girl seemed to calm down. She kept the shutters closed and sat in her room. She was waiting for Mr. Heber. Her bene-factor. Who would arrive punctually around ten in the evening. Having dined with Mrs. Heber.

And now Mrs. Heber went there every day to spy. Mak-ing herself ridiculous. The tenants laughed at her behind her back. They laughed at this housewife who, like them, has nothing to do, and goes around spying on bums. Even the girl began to make fun of Mrs. Heber. Every time she saw her she would pull up her skirt. Or she burst out laugh-ing and then ran off. One day Mrs. Heber gave her a slap. But it's surprising what rapid reflexes you find among half-wits and idiots. As they're called. Or those deprived of their civil rights. The girl threw a punch that made her mouth bleed. And scratched her. They scratched each other. In the middle of the street. Johnny, who as usual was leaning on the wall of the evangelical center, looked on with angelic calm. For once the day was different. That girl had all his mother's strength and energy. For a moment he thought his mother had been reincarnated in the girl. Who was possessed by the devil. He looked on, reveling in the fight. The man who toasted almonds came out into the street too. "They're pretty well killing each other," he said contentedly, and thought of his son. A smile of satisfied revenge spread across his mild face. Everyone saw something from their own past, something far away, that had happened before they came to live in the free house. And waited for the ending. The absolution. The girl opened her bag, pulled out a hammer and struck Mrs. Heber between the eyes. It takes blood to wash away a wrong.

THE PROMISE

THE PROMISE

She'd met her by the snake pit in Berne. And now it was all over. A week later the butcher told her she was looking well, and hoped in his heart that the young lady would keep on spending as she used to. Even the grocer thought she was in good shape. But spinach is too demanding when you're on your own. The grocer knew that, he'd had his shop for more than twenty years and had seen all too many of them *afterwards*. Where there are kids there is hope, for the shop. They eat plenty. But among the couples he referred to as sterile, he knew that *afterwards* purchases drop off. And he knew, as did the butcher for that matter, and the florist, that the two women were a couple. Ruth had passed her off as her sister. But no one believed her. "How's your sister?" they would ask politely. A little lie to make life easier.

She'd begun to look at a girl who was looking at the snakes and seemed to be familiar with some of them. It seemed she called some of them by name. Fritz, Fritz, mein Schatz. She was dressed in a generous skirt and white blouse, flat shoes. Like a student. Her hair was long, straight, blond. Ruth used to go to the zoo on her lunch break too. She would eat a sandwich and then drink a coffee at the snack bar. Behind the snack bar were the toilets. You could hear the din the monkeys made. Ruth didn't like the animals that much. She liked the place as a whole, the wire fences, the enclosures. She liked to go and visit them, without looking at them perhaps, rather than sitting in a café. And that was how she came to be looking at this girl. She had never seen her before. She didn't come every day, but she always came at the same time. And she always stood by the snake pit. Whereas Ruth would walk around, as she did in cemeteries. Among the cages as among the tombstones. She was no longer young and had an oddly precise awareness of the fact. While this girl on the contrary was young. One day she spoke to her and the girl replied very politely. Her name is Vreneli and she comes from a little village in the mountains. Yes, she likes the snakes. She is enthralled.

She was looking for a job and every day she put off the moment when she would ask for work as a cleaner at the zoo. It can't be any harder than doing the cleaning in somebody's house, what did she think? She lived in a room near the station. There were some Portuguese there, some Spaniards. They cooked in their rooms, even though you weren't supposed to. There were two Vietnamese, brother and sister. They used to go out together holding hands till the girl found a job at a dentist's and yesterday the brother had to have his stomach pumped. She wanted to know what Ruth thought. Was it harder to work in someone's house?

Ruth invited her to her house. A little candle-lit dinner for two, with a good wine. She prepared it all herself. The silverware, the crystal glasses, a starched tablecloth. The girl seemed even younger that evening. She had put on a gauzy blue dress with a tight top and plunging neckline. White high heels. As if she were going to her first dance. Ruth was moved. She had brought a modest and moving little bunch of flowers that she held, as though in supplication, in her hand, tied with a ribbon. "I'm glad to be here," she said in a whisper. At the boardinghouse everybody had asked whether she was going to her boyfriend's. And she had confessed, in that same whisper, that she was. She was going to her boyfriend's. Her father and mother were dead. And it was as if she were saying that she didn't have another father and mother. They saw each other again. Vreneli came back to her house, wearing her best dress again. The only one she had for the evening. It was a pleasure for Ruth to buy her a dress. There was a look of bewildered joy in her eyes as she opened the parcel and slipped on the dress. "Turn round, please." Then Ruth was so moved she hugged her.

When they met in the zoo the girl would come skipping towards her. Full of youth. Which Ruth felt she herself had lost for good. Ruth's house was big, it was her parents' house. They had liked big furniture. The wardrobes were big. The wooden bed was big. With big bedside nightstands. Sometimes Ruth kept herself to one half of the bed, her father's. Until a short time ago her father's slippers had still been there in the nightstand, his tobacco tin and pocket watch. Sometimes she slept on her mother's side, and it was as if she could hear her breathing. There were her barrettes in the nightstand. And opposite the bed the heavy dark walnut wardrobe where her grandparents and great-grandparents had hung their clothes. With the passing generations the clothes had taken up more and more space. The old folks never threw anything out. The household gods multiplied. There in the wardrobe, in the shadow of the hangers, that's where my life will be, she had thought. The evening dresses to go dancing, the smart suits for travel, because she would travel of course, and marry. But when she imagined her husband's clothes hanging there too, she blanched. Her parents and theirs before them would have liked her to marry. They even told her as much as they lay dying, held her hand beneath their own, death-pale. They imagined words carried more weight when spoken at death's door. And they died happy. Ruth had promised.

Ruth was nineteen at the time and went on thinking about her promise. She let a school friend have her. After their night together she muttered a thank you, then kept out of his way. She let Mr. Erni have her, who owned the biggest pastry shop in the canton, for a couple of nights. She let a tourist have her. But then said enough is enough. She had done her duty. She had honored her promise. As far as possible. Three men had passed over her body, the same way her father passed over her mother's no doubt. She liked sleeping alone, sometimes her feet were cold, she liked waking alone, and so wanted to be alone when her eyelids closed. Her work was well paid. She worked in a lawyer's office. And the law was her prayer book.

One evening she showed Vreneli the bedroom. Vreneli immediately lay down like a child, her muslin dress rode up to her stomach. "Sorry," she said. She sat on the bed, polite and shy. That evening she didn't go back to the boarding-house. And she never went back, for thirty-two years. She slept on the window-side and Ruth on her father's side. A few days later Ruth went through Vreneli's bag and saw her I.D. She wasn't young at all. She was thirty-seven, almost the same age as Ruth. Ruth was forty-two. But Vreneli went on playing the little girl for years. She kept house, cooked, did the shopping. When Ruth came back from work, she lit up with joy. They rarely argued. When they did, Ruth told her she was old. "Old like me." Vreneli's eyes brimmed with tears. She was hurt. She sat in a corner, wouldn't speak, lips clamped shut.

There came a time, which lasted about five years, when Vreneli would go out on her own of an evening as soon as Ruth had fallen asleep. It wasn't clear where she went. When she came back her hair was mussed and some mornings Ruth would see marks on her neck, later covered by a silk scarf. She never asked her anything. In the end, she wasn't upset about it. What did upset her was to see some of her parents' things disappearing. Silverware. Of course, poor Vreneli was hardly young now, she said as much to her one

evening, and perhaps had to pay someone for whatever at-
tentions she enjoyed. Her hair had turned white, though
she dyed it blond. Her body didn't thicken out. At home
she wandered about in a dressing gown cinched at the waist,
short enough to show her legs. In the parents' big bed
Vreneli was affectionate, sometimes she overdid it with the
perfume, and, if Ruth's feet were cold, she would stroke
them and kiss them and warm them with her hair, which
she still wore long down her back.

Ruth was neither cheered nor irritated by her aging
girlfriend. Sometimes she would speak to her parents and
tell them that her marriage had been a success. After all,
even her father used to go out at night. But that had never
upset their married life. He had been discreet, as was
Vreneli. And if Vreneli stole a thing or two it was only because she still didn't think of herself as one of the family,
Ruth's wife, in which case what belonged to Ruth would
have belonged to her too. So for a few years Vreneli chose
to steal. For although everything was shared, it all came
from Ruth and her parents. From kith and kin. "It all belongs to you," Vreneli would say. And in a sweet, shy voice
muttered: "Even the bank account." Every week, or whenever Vreneli asked, Ruth gave her some money. Ruth de-
cided that to celebrate Vreneli's sixtieth birthday, she would
open a bank account for her. One May morning they went
to the bank and for the first time since they started living
together Vreneli signed her own name, her real name. Not
the name of the imaginary sister, as she did when the post-
man brought a parcel or a registered letter.

She still hadn't got used to the fact that the janitor of the building where they lived would use Ruth's second name when he greeted her. "Guten Tag, Fräulein Meyer." She was Fräulein Hess. They went to the Balearic Islands, the Antilles, to places photographed in tourist brochures, and Vreneli whispered that they looked like photographs themselves, in their summer clothes.

They were just heaping up memories. She, Vreneli, wants to stay at home and remember, not to experience the memories themselves. Did Ruth understand this? Vreneli was getting awkward. Memories and grime. She didn't bother with the housework, the dust thickened on the furniture, the mirrors grew dull. Only at night did the house rediscover its old splendor. Vreneli lit candles, the flames burned in the mirrors, as on that first evening. The days became insubstantial, the night immediately there to be touched.

Right to the end she still wanted new dresses. Confined to her bed, she would stroke them with her hands. She chose the dress she was to wear to her grave. After a great deal of hesitation. She discussed the matter at length with Ruth. It was a pleasure to choose that dress. Vreneli seemed happy with her choice and at peace with herself. She made Ruth promise she wouldn't take off her satin shoes. She wanted to be buried in the Meyer family tomb. It was her right, she said. And there was room in the Meyer family tomb. Because Ruth hadn't married and hadn't had children. Who would have had their places. "And what will the Meyers do?" Vreneli went on, worried. "They'll be angry."

Ruth must make sure that her coffin was hermetically sealed. Perhaps, she suggested, an iron coffin would be better, like a suit of armor. Ruth smiled. She said: "We'll be nothing but worms, dear, dust." "Oh, worms. . . ." Vreneli smiled too. Her blue eyes fluttered evasively.

There was a commotion in the house the following morning. Once the formalities and simple burial were over, Ruth opened the iron gate of the family tomb and didn't leave until every letter of the name had been engraved: Vreneli Meyer Hess.

PORZIA

PORZIA

When the accident happened, Doris Bechtler was lying awake in her bed waiting for her goodnight kiss. She wasn't feeling well disposed towards these parents who had forgotten her. She was wearing a pink nightdress, in her pink bedroom. It had always been her favorite colour and even now at twenty-four she always wore pink in bed. Lips pressed tight in disappointment, she looked like a little girl still. Whenever she heard a noise, she would get ready to lift her arms, because when her mother and father came in to say goodnight she would hug them warmly and eagerly around their necks. She'd done the same as a tiny child when her small arms were as neatly turned as a cherub's. And her parents' hugs were fierce too, often her mother would draw her so tightly to herself it seemed she meant to suffocate her.

The night we're talking about she was once again looking forward to that embrace, for every day seemed the last
somehow. Some say youth is when our ruin takes root. That
certainly wasn't true of Doris Bechtler. Youth and infancy
were still inviolate in her, in both body and soul. Of course
her body has undergone its changes. The little girl is big
now, but that is all. Her eyes stare into the dark, willful and
menacing. Her gaze settled on the memory of the last few
hours. She had gone into the big bedroom, her mother was
sitting at her dresser, in front of the oval mirror. In the mirror were her mother's face, neck, and bare shoulders. Doris
had struck up a pose behind her, as if for a photograph, resting a hand on one shoulder. She would have liked to stay in
the picture a little longer, those last few moments of her
preparations. Her mother's face and hair were ready and
Doris was allowed to enter the mirror, fasten her pearl necklace, and admire its beauty. "You're perfect, Mutti." Her
mother jumped up—she was always late for something—
and hurried off. Doris would watch her body loom up in the
mirror, then disappear in haste. The mirror was left empty
and superfluous.

The bulldog barks. Doris opens the window. The dog is
pacing nervously up and down inside a generous, wire-
fenced enclosure. The moon is full and the lake is resting
quietly. Or almost. It looks blighted. Doris puts on her pink
dressing gown and swishes from her room into the passage,
she knocks at her parents' door, enters on tiptoe, finding
nothing on the bed but her mother's nightgown, laid out
like an effigy on the piqué coverlet. On the other side of the

bed are pajama pants and an unbuttoned bedjacket. The first light slipping into the room shows the two fetishes waiting to be occupied. Porzia is the artist behind these posturing nightclothes, and has been ever since Doris's mother first saw her nightgown lying on the bed and said to Porzia: "It looks like me, it's as if I were there."

Porzia took it as a compliment and ever since—for it's twenty-five years since Mr. and Mrs. Bechtler were married—she has been arranging her mistress's nightgown as if it were alive. Porzia came from a village in Val Brembana, near Bergamo. She didn't speak a word of German, but quickly learnt the Swiss variety.

When Doris, the only daughter, was born, Porzia was able to sing her lullabies in Swiss German. She was the same age as her mistress, but scarcely full of life. She had little appetite for free time or amusement. She would sit on a bench by the lake, as if ordered to. Sometimes she would go to church and kneel. Rather than an altar it was the lake she felt she was seeing. She doesn't pray. But anyone watching would have thought her extremely devout. Intensely withdrawn, as though walled up in herself, with a misty, malignant look. An ancestral violence in her eyes, perhaps her forebears were no better than prey for carnivores. Such was Porzia in her free time, Thursday and Sunday afternoons. When she came back home, to her employers' house, she resumed her everyday expression, all visions consigned to the void. The soft green of her eyes recovered its light. A polite smile. "Where have you been, Porzia?" her mistress would ask. In a lakeside town one inevitably goes down to the lake to stare at the water. Porzia allowed herself to be haunted by what she had stared at. She couldn't tear her eyes away, they went right to the lake bottom. She was haunted by dead things. Porzia was pleasantly stocky, with her raven hair cropped short she looked like a boy. Mrs. Bechtler was sure that Porzia was a virgin. "Wouldn't you like to get married and have a family?" she asked once. "Nein," Porzia answered simply. And she stuck by that no. She didn't want a family of her own and when she took little Doris out in her pram, and ran with the pram along the lakefront in Zurich, she had already forgotten her family near Bergamo, her sour old parents, for that little girl who sometimes called her "Mutti" by mistake. And even now that Doris was a young woman she didn't treat her as a servant, but *almost* as a mother. "You are my old mother," she would say. "But I'm the same age as your mother." "You are much older than her, because you were already old."

What the girl meant was that Porzia was a good witch who came from far away and had become young again by magic. Because she was a witch. The girl told her how once she had gone into her room and found a lock of her own hair in the drawer in the nightstand. Only a witch would keep my hair in a drawer, Doris had thought.

The girl grew up with apprehensions of what was true and what was almost so. And now, lying in her bed, she was very angry with her parents. They know she can't get to sleep without her goodnight kiss. Towards four in the morning Porzia came into the room. She sits by the bed. Her mother and father wouldn't be coming back. The girl, the young woman, shouted angrily. She demands that Porzia explain why they haven't given her her goodnight kiss. That's the only thing that matters. For a moment Porzia thinks she must have gone mad. Has she really not understood that her parents are dead? They found them in the lake, she said, spelling it out. If that is so, if that corresponds to the truth, Doris wants to see them. She will, thinks Porzia, in their two coffins, laid out, faces spread with gauze. Porzia strokes the girl. Exhausted by the news and the shock, eyelids exhausted, she falls asleep. Perhaps it's almost true, they are dead. Porzia stays a moment longer in the room until the breathing becomes regular and quiet.

After the appropriate formalities, the funeral. In the Protestant chapel of the Zurich city cemetery Doris listened to the sermon of Pastor Anton, who had baptized her. Meantime the smoke climbed into the sky. They were burning, it was spring. Her parents had been truly proud of her, Anton was saying. When the ceremony was over, Doris thanked the clergyman and invited him to the funeral reception. Doris had chosen the flowers for the chapel, but not the menu. That was written in the will. Her parents had even stipulated what hors d'oeuvres were to be served and the order of the wines. The sole beneficiary asked herself, somewhat resentfully, why on earth her parents had given instructions for the reception. What's more, they had given instructions as to which cars were to be sent for which guests. This too was written in the will. As if the only thing that had mattered to her parents was that funeral reception, immediately after the ceremony. Doris had been able to decide about the flowers in the chapel, the flowers not being mentioned in the will. And Doris was sparing. There was no grand show in the chapel, they were timorous flowers, pretty and shy.

She had been a long time at the florist. Porzia stood behind her and made no comment. She was wearing an old black overcoat and a waterproof hat, black shoes with rather squarish toes. "It's just vanity," Doris said out loud. The wreaths. Porzia's eyelids flutter in agreement. Then she goes up to her and says that thinking it vanity is just a prejudice and . . . But Doris immediately answers that she is not prejudiced and the strong smell of the flowers was making her sick. They are already rotting. And then it seemed to her that the flowers were very expensive. Even though she was rich, she wasn't used to spending. Now the sole beneficiary is amazed to find how much things cost. Her sharp eyes glare at the yellow roses.

She had never had anything to do with money. Now she must decide how much money to spend on the flowers in the Protestant chapel. The funeral cars, she suspected, were very expensive. And likewise the restaurant. But there she must bow to her parents' wishes. She studied the previous months' accounts like a school textbook, to get an idea how much it costs to live. She wasn't in the least surprised by the size of her fortune. Now everything belongs to her: the dead, the property, and a large share, she reflected, of nothingness. Porzia made herself useful. She was familiar, one might have said, with the invisible wishes of Mr. and Mrs. Bechtler. Porzia tried to explain to Doris that it was her duty to offer a lunch, an excellent lunch, to all those who came. An unforgettable lunch, said Porzia. As for paragraph three, the paragraph that gave instructions for the funeral, Doris scrupulously observed her parents' desires. Which might well have been Porzia's too. Sitting at Mr. Bechtler's desk, the young lady and Porzia went through the accounts until Doris yawned. It was so boring, and death seemed boring too. On top of everything else she would have to answer all the letters of condolence, of deeply felt condolence. She asked Porzia to do it. And Porzia was more than happy to help her little girl who didn't feel like saying thank you. "Don't leave anyone out, Porzia, Mutti always used to write a letter whenever anyone died. And she didn't feel like going to the funeral." Porzia got to work sitting at Mr. Bechtler's desk, at night, while Doris slept, having nothing more to worry about. She had already done a great deal. She had spoken words of consolation to guests sincerely upset by her parents' death. Both at the same time. In her room Porzia hadn't yet undressed. She sat up a long time, thinking. She opened the drawer of the nightstand and from the bottom pulled out the wooden cross, the only thing she had brought with her from Italy. They had placed it in her dying mother's hands and at the last moment Porzia had taken it. Almost without thinking, she had put it in her pocket. And on the train to Zurich she had fingered the thing, without pulling it out of her pocket. She felt it had been profaned and didn't want any of the other passengers to see it. But now she has it in her hand. She raises it to the ceiling. The thing is charged with darkness. Then she puts the cross on the bed, in the middle of the bed, where she imagines her mother's hands were arranged in that other bed. Porzia stole the cross. She wanted to make sense of it all. She has never been religious. But now this cross seemed to be speaking to her. Prompting her thoughts. The cross was about five inches long and bore no Savior. It was just a cross. The cross, she thinks, accompanies all the dead on their journey. It lies there motionless like a sleeping scorpion. She feels this object conceals the sap of her secret thoughts. Stealing it was sacrilege. You can't steal from the dead—and her mother had smiled, as if, already in night's other kingdom, she sensed she had the blessed cross beside her. "Look," someone had said, "your mother is smiling." Sometimes—she knew, she'd seen it in animals—they had a muscle spasm afterwards, a nervous contraction.

At last she took off her black coat. She was hot. She opened the window. Thick clouds scudded across the moon and the light would slip into her room, then fade, like her intermittent thoughts. She was overcome by a damp warmth, the spring was already sultry. Now she knows why she stole the cross. The theft of the cross established her niche. She had stolen this object of faith from the smooth cold hands—that's what one says of hands—in a trance almost. She hadn't planned to do it, but she'd wanted to take from the old woman's hands what mattered most to her, to punish her. To spite her, just for once. She had always been obedient and well behaved. She did the milking, because she was told to. And found it repugnant, she didn't like animals, she wanted to serve a human being. Around her for the most part were animals, her parents, a few children. A few children who tortured lizards and rabbits. Porzia was kind to the animals, but didn't want to work with them. She did the milking. Gloomily, brooding. One day she would up and off. To find human beings.

The hens in the coop were her friends. She could see them transformed into women. Chicken feet in high heels and they pulled eggs out of their handbags. But when their throats were torn out, by stray dogs, or wolves or foxes, she said they were just hens. They shouted at her, it was her fault for leaving the door open. All that blood was her fault. The children jeered at her for letting the hens and chickens get killed, but their eyes were brimming with amazement and joy. Nothing else happened in those parts. On the train she felt free, looking out at a landscape she would never see again. Was there any sense, then, in her having stolen the cross? Now Porzia understood. She'd had it in her pocket when Frau Bechtler took her on and felt the wood fretting against her hip. They were both eighteen years old. Now Frau Bechtler was dead, together with her husband. They died in a car accident. The wooden cross placed in her mother's joined hands had taken its revenge. Faith, thought Porzia, and sacred objects are ever vengeful.

In the ground, Porzia's mother would have gone on adoring that piece of wood. She even used to thank it when the hens were killed, though the fault was Porzia's. Porzia had made sure her mother would do no praying, in the ground. By stealing the cross, she had taken life from the life that was no more. She's desperate, Porzia thought, now she can't worship that piece of wood anymore.

In the days following the funeral, Alfred, the parents' bulldog, would go up to their bedroom and whine. Doris tried to talk to him. He mustn't make that noise. She said it sweetly, with that sweetness a master or mistress sometimes shows to an inferior. She was sad enough as it was at losing her parents, she didn't want another to sing counterpoint to her grief. Which was what Alfred was doing. Alfred pricked up his ears and listened. Doris shut her parents' door, left the room exactly as it had been, the silk spread out on the bed and the husband's pajamas on the other side. Doris told the dog to look at her when she spoke to him and Alfred raised his paw, which Doris immediately took hold of. Friends again, Alfred understood. Doris was relieved that Porzia was cold and contrite and behaved as though nothing had happened. At table there was only one person to serve instead of three, the young lady. But Alfred's grief was far too effusive. Next day he managed to get into their room on the first floor and started whining again. Doris beat him with his leash. The bulldog snarled. Did he mean to be more moved than she was? She gave the creature to an elderly couple who had a house with a garden in Meilen. The elderly couple then poisoned the dog. Porzia had gone with Doris to see them. The couple—they looked like brother and sister—were enjoying the feeble sunshine in their garden, eyelids half-closed, but aware of what was going on outside the garden. Both very tall, they bent over the dog, studying it. Eyes shiny with emotion, they said: "He'll keep us company." "We are so lonely, Fräulein Bechtler," said the old woman, with a rather stubborn squeak. Having studied the animal in silence, walking round and round it, they invited the young lady and Porzia into their house. They offered a glass of water. They sit down and a chary conversation begins. Both are lean and lanky. The old man has short grey prickly hair while his wife's hangs straight to the nape of the neck. The old woman drinks her water slowly. She moves her lips, lets out a sudden yell, shrill and wild: "My grandson is so pretty." Then she falls silent. "He's up there." A bony hand points to the mantelpiece. The photograph is silver-framed. Porzia and Doris look up. "He's a pretty boy," they say. The woman moves her lips to smile. "They all say he looks like a girl," she mutters bitterly. Once again her brow is heavy with silence. But now it's the man who speaks. He comes out with his words one by one, as if he were counting them. They only have a few more years to enjoy the house and garden. And the little boy who looks like a girl. His eyes glaze over. Time is short. They have made their sacrifices, but sacrifices are never returned. That's a law of science. It made them sad. The boy who looks like a girl angelically displays small teeth, yellow curls, sky blue eyes, painted mouth, rosy cheeks, like thousands upon thousands of little girls. He's there on the mantelpiece, waiting to become more masculine perhaps, though he doesn't look overly concerned about it. Even better, thinks Porzia, if he were to stay so pretty forever.

Earthly desires run deep in these old folks. The man insists that he wants to see the boy grow up, until his voice breaks. He sees nothing else, the rest of the world is a mere disturbance. A real dog, like this bulldog called Alfred, will help the boy to grow up, spur him on to become a man. Something the stuffed and plastic animals that cram his room can never do. They are everywhere. The old folks feel suffocated in that room with those stupid toys. The bulldog is real.

*　　*　　*

The seasons come and go and Doris is sitting in the armchair her father once sat in. She wallowed in grief. Everything is silent. Doris heard nothing. Not even the faint soft trembling of the lace curtains as they seem to breathe in the breeze. So they are gone. She spent hours and hours on the deck chair, on the lawn by the lake. Thinking. One feels fine in this world, when one lacks for nothing. How fine she felt, even though her parents were dead. She was mistress of the house. Mistress of the empty house and the garden, but also mistress of her parents. When others die we become their masters and mistresses, their guardians up to a point. It has never occurred to her that the opposite might be true, that perhaps our lives are governed by them.

When it was foggy, the lake shone burnished silver and the garden settled in the water. It looked like a marsh where the dead roam. Only one living being breathed that air, herself. The wrought-iron table, where they used to eat in summer, was covered with leaves, and silent now, like everything else in the garden. All the words they had spoken to each other were gone. Likewise that special timbre that lives on after a calamity, crystalline almost, for some time, and then is at last submerged, crushed under an immense shroud. At first, not long after they were dead, when the bereavement was fresh, she would hear their voices. The voices of her father and mother. Peach ice cream on the table. Raspberries, red currants, the purple of the bilberries. Slow, monotonous voices speaking dialect. Scars appeared on the garden's yellow roses. On her birthday her parents would invite other children over for a trip on the lake, in their motorboat. Doris was bored. The motorboat is still in the boathouse. Cobwebs cover the windows. Haunted by child ghosts, their laughter, their happy birthday, insect laughter, threads, and claws within. The motorboat floats as though in a bog, asleep, in a stench of evil water.

She thought she saw a light in her parents' room, closed for years now. She rushed in. Alfred's mad and melancholy eyes stared at her. So she thought. He was crouching on the floor. She tried to stroke him, but he ran off. Doris regretted having punished him for his funereal whining. She was sorry she had given him to that old couple. And she told him as much, looking for him everywhere, but the dog was gone. "It can't be Alfred," she thinks. "It was those eyes tricked me." She shouldn't have felt sorry at all. Came the sound of Porzia's voice. She'd done well to get rid of Alfred. "I am Alfred. I crouched on the floor. The rest is credulity." Doris knew perfectly well that Alfred had been poisoned by those old people. Did Doris believe, by any chance, in the resurrection? And Porzia laughed. As she had never laughed in her life. It was she who had howled, she who had possessed Alfred's spirit, the spirits of the Bechtlers, as she would possess Doris's spirit too. Porzia's mad and melancholy eyes exulted in the flames that crinkled the curtains as though for a ball. In her hand she held something black that wouldn't burn. Ritual objects will have their revenge.

THE TWINS

THE TWINS

The village has no name. There's a church, fenced in by the dead, a dozen or so houses, the barns and the Schübeli twins' broken-down cottage. If a traveler should pass by, and it's a rare occurrence, he stops to look at the graves. All stone but one, carved in wood that looks like leather. And how could the traveler know that behind curtained windows hard, sharp eyes are watching him? In the distance, a muffled sound: scythes. People shouldn't poke into their cemetery. It's like poking into their houses. Strangers even walk into their tiny gardens. A notice warns: Do not touch the flowers. In the German-speaking regions of the Alps flowers bud and blossom in furious haste, only to wither slowly, lazily. They too seem unhappy about strangers, for they change color at the approach of eyes from other worlds, as if seized by frenzy. When the hay is gathered in, all the meadow flowers are mowed down, perhaps prematurely. Having snipped off some anemone stalks and made them at home in a glass under the glare of an electric light, a poet compared their demeanor and gesturing to the abandonment of Saint Teresa as imagined by Bernini. Gravestones and flowers are mutinous creatures. Creatures? It's not nice for a bunch of flowers to be tightly twined in leaden lace. Nor even in pleated paper that holds them as though in a ruff. Ruffs look well in a Rembrandt portrait, against a dark background.

The wooden grave that looks like leather belongs to the Schübeli family. The names weren't etched in the wood, but seem to have been written with ink. Or black blood. "Oh to be able to admire simple things," travelers would say. "Death is simple: a flower bed, a dead name. And the glare, the silence, summer and winter." An old man goes by with a pitchfork. At the windows only geraniums and lace curtains watch him pass. Behind the curtains, eyes. The villagers keep their eyes hidden, it's the houses and the wood that stare. Only the old men with their old wives and St. Bernards were left. The children had gone—from the beginning it seemed. No trace of them now. As if, in the order of things, memories were superfluous and contemptible. And for those old mountain folk children had been a joy and an oblivion. The oblivion proved the stronger. These people had understood that the essence of life lies in limitation. Or omission. When the twins, Hans and Ruedi, arrived on a gig they were welcomed with stern satisfaction. Together with the old folk, the first thing Hans and Ruedi did was to go to visit their parents in the cemetery. They doffed their caps, their hair shining gold. "Thank you," they both said. They thanked their parents for the cottage they had inherited. The old people showed them other graves. The twins saluted the dead. Before each stone Hans and Ruedi bowed their heads, it was a social occasion. A presentation at Court. A bow before the souls. Hans and Ruedi were identical. Ruedi had one blue eye and one brown. Hans's were both brown. That was how you could tell them apart. Bundles on their backs held all their belongings: spare socks, a suit of black cloth, Bible, and boots, tied up with a lace. They are eighteen years old. There's mold in the cottage and a cup broken exactly in two. As though it were the mark of their destiny: they would glue it together, united like their own lives. But then each took a half, threw it on the ground and stamped on it. Hooks hung from low beams. Why haven't they hung anything there? Not even a goat? Now they can say whatever they think. Without a taste of poison in their mouths. "Go now," they told the old folk. Hans and Ruedi had left the other orphans, their companions in misfortune, only a few hours before. The institute was financed by the Confederation. Their misfortune was not so much being orphaned, but, as the twins saw it, having to wait until they came of age before taking possession of the house. Their house of origin, they called it. The house where a dead woman had given birth to them. They dreamt of it. They felt homesick for this place they had never known and were forever talking about it. The orphanage inflicted goodness and charity. The charity that merely perpetuates poverty. They had grown wild, felt no affection for anyone. There weren't many orphans in the Confederation. Some had found a family. Hans and Ruedi made sure that no one wanted them, saw affection as their worst enemy. They didn't want to be split up. Well-to-do couples had already adopted Koreans, Filipinos, Indians, but were afraid of the twins. The twins want to return to a place they don't remember. The place, they would say, of imagination. Not bonds of kinship, which they no longer have, nor generosity, nor the friendship of their companions, who would sink exhausted in their beds at night and sleep soundly. Some boys wanted to play with the twins, and bothered them. They were imagining their house. Playing with the others, they felt, brought bad luck. They played, to put it simply, with the hereafter, in a sensible way. During their half-hour breaks all Hans and Ruedi wanted was to walk about holding hands and sit beside each other. They were hostile to the guardians of the law, and all forms of brutality. They were happier at fourteen when they became pantry boys. They were treated as workers. They were quits with charity. They had left infancy behind them. They had left corruption behind them. Their games brought a salary. At sixteen they join the church and receive Confirmation. They are dressed in black. Adults. They like ceremony. They were impressed by the biscuit-colored stucco figures. The angels were frivolous. Confirmation day was a holiday. It seemed long to the twins. They spent the whole day on their beds, dressed in black. "How well-behaved they are," thought the old folk, as the twins bowed their heads over the tombstones.

Hans and Ruedi sleep on a mattress on the floor. Then they build a very large bed. They inlay the headboard with berries, bunches of grapes, and diamond shapes. Having finished that, they never go anywhere else. Only once, when they'd already been there a year, did they go to town to buy a radio. They wanted to listen to a bit of music of an evening. They danced. In winter the village was buried in snow. Early in the morning Hans and Ruedi shoveled a path to the old folks' doors. The old folks were getting lazy. They were happy to watch the two boys born from the dead woman, to see them so strong and animal-like almost. They worked with wood. They made medieval chairs, barbaric, heavy things, and a long table. They sat at each end of the table. The glasses were tall, the plates large, the ceilings low. And, since there was plenty of wood, they started on coffins. As with the head of the bed, they gave free reign to their artistic flare. They inlaid the coffins with crosses, cocks, bunches of grapes, spheres. The old folks came and admired them—and would want the finest. Hans and Ruedi carved inlaid landscapes too. Carried away, they began to paint. Tropical landscapes, rhinoceroses, snakes, animals with human heads. They hid the cross among scales. The tropical landscape sat well with the snow that buried the village. "Where did you see all this?" the old folks would ask. In the kitchen. When they were washing the dishes, dreaming of their house of origin, they would see it full of figures. In the dirty water they saw faces melt into each other. And clouds

.

too. Their masters were clouds and bogs. It was a lucky village. A cable car brought up everything they needed. And the pastor too, with his wife. For the services, when he could, snow and avalanches permitting.

It was a bright Sunday morning in February when the pastor shouted in the chapel. It was one of the days his wife came and perhaps because it was unusually mild she had donned a spring bonnet. "Pagans!" the pastor shouted. Sitting next to the twins, his wife had never heard him shout before. Even her bonnet trembled. The feather had a fit of shivers. She had never heard him shout. In twenty-five years of marriage. The pastor invariably spoke softly, and she, used as she was to raising her voice with the farmyard animals, would have trouble hearing him. In the early years of their marriage, when she was serving him stew, she would ask him in a loud voice whether he wanted a second helping and stand there ladle in hand. "Noch einmal?" "More?" She was used to speaking in a loud voice. The man murmured: "Don't shout," and she would stand there waiting to hear if he wanted a second helping or not. She felt hurt. A flush of shy, sulky anger rose in her cheeks. Immediately she lowered her voice, and so with the passing years the wife too had come to whisper. As if speaking was an insult.

As the pastor saw it the twins were damned. "They are savages," he said. The old folk, about ten were still alive, listened unperturbed. He had never been expansive, they thought, in his services, or when giving last rites. They were familiar with his scanty words and silences, an avid tightness about his mouth when someone gave way to a moment's emotion as the earth clattered on a relative. His wife found it hard, though at forty it had seemed like providence when he asked for her hand in marriage. And now Pastor Brandl is being asked to give last rites to the St. Bernard. It was the custom once, the old folks said. In the mountains. The wife winced. She hadn't been married long to the pastor when she would have liked her husband to read a verse or two over little Eveline, but she hadn't dared. The cat had been such a good friend. It had laid its little paw on her arm to thank her for all her care. The pastor put the animal in a plastic bag. Without looking at it. It was the wife's duty to take out the garbage. And she disinfected the kitchen too. As Brandl saw it, death is pestilence, is filth. "Pagans!" he shouted again.

She went to the taxidermist's store in Chur. Among the half-live heads of other animals she tried to find the cat that had been tossed in the garbage. She was looking for a relation, among the foxes and condors perhaps. "We don't embalm cats, lady," said the offended storekeeper. "Not in Chur." But they do still embalm, thought the pastor's wife, which was enough for her. Sometimes she felt guilty when she tiptoed into her husband's silent office, for he would punish her for the tiniest thing. And what punishment would he have inflicted if he had so much as an inkling of her visits to the embalmers, to the store that resurrects that which is vain. After much hesitation she bought an owl. It seemed warm when she held it in her arms. She covered it with old rags and hid it in a cupboard. She was struck by the bird's imperiously empty gaze as she covered it up and hid it away. All day long she felt those eyes following her, their iciness.

She was possessed by a great energy. Now she can protect herself from her husband. She tiptoed into his study to serve him his café crème and biscuits. The pastor thanked her without opening his mouth. "Nicht zu danken," she says for the first time. "No need to thank me." She would undo the stuffed bird's rags. His thanks had once been a kind of salvation, but she could do without them now. The woman has ceased to atone for things, and if atonement is a movement of the soul, she has ceased to have one, that thing her husband keeps in his dark, purply gums. And which, until the fatal day she married, she'd thought lay in the heart. Souls need neither prayers nor words. It's secrecy they want. A wreath of yellow flowers framed the St. Bernard's enormous head. The old folks brought him food in a wooden bowl. Hans and Ruedi stroked him with white kid gloves. "Pagans!" Brandl shouted for the last time, and fell silent. He fell silent before the dog's enormous head. He wished that vultures might strip the flesh from its head, and from the twins too. He had never been a violent man, never had such brutal thoughts, and since to his mind thoughts were the only manifestation of the truth, he was afraid. He wished a carcass dead. He had attacked the dog with a stick. He beat it. "Why attack something that's dead, Father?" the twins asked together. The twins were like officiants at some rite. They're smiling. They repeat their question in wheedling voices. Had the dead thing snarled perhaps? They took Brandl's stick from him and snapped it in two.

Objects of violence, they said, are easily snapped, Father. See, it's so easy to have violent thoughts. Brandl wished the twins might be torn to pieces. Torn to pieces by dead things. He imagined the tropical landscape the twins had painted coming alive. Trophies of poison and sorrow. He saw saints' faces, tracings, masks. The dark green of the gloom made shadows seem palpable, suffocating bodies.

He thought of his stern desk with its dark wood, of his spare, comfortable study where he would sit preparing his sermons. He thought for a long time. Murmuring. "The word is made incarnate but no one notices." His hands closed tight on nothingness. Then leaned on his knees. The light catches his profile, glasses on the tip of his nose, eyelids lowered, feet together in long heavy shoes. This man is Pastor Brandl, as he imagined he looked. And not that fellow shouting. The pages of his Bible turned over on their own, stirred by martial blasts of wind in the dimly lit room, as he went on and on thinking of what he would say, how he would put together his sermon. Truth notwithstanding, he always felt he must invent. And he had misgivings. He had misgivings with regard to the Bible—and how not to have them? He had passionate misgivings with regard to the Holy Scriptures, to the knowledge of the absolute and its unfolding in fable.

Tone of voice was important to him. He must have been horrified to hear himself shout. As though existence were but a sequence of voices, a back and forth of low, steady, well-educated voices. Until at last a voice shouted, beside itself, as if possessed. When he preached, his voice was monotonous, slow, he laid no stress on the words—and his congregation liked it that way. The sound of that shout torments him. Lost. It was all over now. And the day was getting at once sharper and more ephemeral. Over a trifle. What on earth can it mean to give last rites to a St. Bernard? You can't give last rites to a lettuce, can you? You can't say a prayer over a mere outward appearance. Markets are full of fruit and greens and flowers, but it would never occur to you to administer last rites to those decapitations, would it? Those phantasmagoria? A kind thought. He remembered the Crawford Market in Bombay: the colors of the vegetables were as if drunk, raising hymns to glory. The merchants slept. Their day was over when the sun reached the zenith. So high the spirit can never go there perhaps—it would be blinded. A smell of spices, desires, fumes, the animals in their cages, the fruits of the earth in the grandiose spasm of ultimate theatricality. An exhausting smell. It was a mocking, gluttonous *vanitas*. Black sacks in the middle. Other sleepers on the sacks. The merchants' sleep and the prayerful light beneath Victorian flourishes. Sinuous bodies, dressed in rags, likewise had a theatrical shape. Bones, blood, and mind. Drooping eyelids, glimpsed eyes. Far more than the words what mattered to Pastor Brandl was the tone of voice. In his thoughts, then, the time of mortification had come. He must punish himself. And he must punish his thoughts. Thoughts find no forgiveness. He himself was becoming a thought. It may be that a thought doesn't have a physical shape, but Brandl felt the physical shape of thought upon him. He thought he was seeing himself in a mirror.

Whoever wishes evil on others feels evil within himself. Brandl, the meek and charitable pastor, with reservations, has never had dealings with the dust of goodness. "Dust," he said out loud. Thoughts have little need to be thought. But came anyway. Goodness is nothing but dust and illusion, everything becomes something else, goodness inflicts evil. Brandl was delirious. Everything proceeded rationally, even things that seemed irrational. Brandl wiped his forehead with a carefully ironed white linen handkerchief. How tiresome sweat can be. They saw him run north, trip on a stone, fall, and spring up again. He fell and got up again a number of times. Then they looked away. They forgot him. The sun was sinking, having kindled perpetual snows. It split the landscape in two, half leaden, half a dying fire. Left the shadows to their triumph.

*   *   *

The twins shut the doors. In winter they shovel away the snow. One night they made love together and felt a little ashamed. They'd never done it when they were young. They'd been distractedly chaste. Now in their old age, as if it were a commandment from above, the twins felt they must know each other in the Biblical sense. Just once. They came together. Intoxicated. It was a spiritual fury, they said afterwards, and each apologized to the other. The years flew softly by.

The days grew shorter. Early afternoon became evening. They got up earlier and earlier in the morning. They looked at each other and, having checked they were alive, felt happy. "You awake, Hans?" "You awake, Ruedi?" Sometimes they don't want to sleep, for fear they might not wake up again. They lie in the big bed with its inlaid headboard, gazing at the tiny windows, holding hands, gripping each other's wrists. They remembered when they'd been pantry boys, children. And their companions in misfortune, ghosts they seemed now. Misfortune looked like a gift from God. A painless misfortune. That was what it was.

And now? They are tough, they have an excess of strength, they say, which gives rise to melancholy. They have too much physical strength, that's why they've grown melancholic. Perhaps they don't know what melancholy means. They've never heard the word. Not even on the radio. They listen to music. Is it a malignant disease? Being melancholic, they shovel quite furiously. They even shovel where there's no need. This winter they were sure they'd come to the end. They're disappointed. Spring grins at the windows. And when dawn came a light tinged faintly yellow betrayed the eternity of another day. They eat in silence. Chewing slowly. Chewing with nothing in their mouths. They have fallen prey to a sort of futile, obstinate melancholy. In the passageway by the front door were the army-issue rifle, the spade, and the pitchfork. Three useful things.

"Want me to kill you?" says Hans. "Want me to kill you?" says Ruedi. No, they don't want that. They shave carefully. They iron their shirts, starching cuffs and collars. Stiffening them. They wear dark suits, the same ones they wore for their Confirmation. They were too big then and now they fit perfectly. They go for a walk in the village. They walked by empty houses, bowing their heads as they passed shuttered windows. Only the façade is left. There was something sweet in the air. God knows where from.

The Alps were veiled in hush and deceit and the brilliant colors of the gentians shone on their squat stalks. A woman knocked at the twins' house that day. No sooner was she in the door than she produced an I.D. from her shiny black shoulder bag. The twins didn't look at it. From the corner of their eyes they saw the word "Police." The woman was from the Pro Senectute. She said she wanted to protect them. From old age and death. What airs she gives herself, they thought. They invited her to take a seat. They, these gentlemen, could no longer go on living alone in this house. And in an abandoned village to boot. They must move to a holiday home near Chur. "Holiday?" the twins said together. "Yes, holiday." They nodded, eyes half-closed in an expression of pity. There they would find friends to talk to and play cards with. "But we don't play cards." The lady insisted it was quite natural to want to play before passing on to the other world. They must find something to take death off their minds. She promised them a terrestrial paradise before moving on to the celestial version, all expenses paid by the Confederation. As orphans, she went on, the gentlemen had already been taken under the wing of the Confederation. They will be protected. Those who have been in orphanages are taken back when they reach a certain age. Did they understand? She shook their hands vigorously and said she would be back. There were some documents for them to sign.

As soon as they were left alone, the twins started to think it over. Did Hans want a holiday before he died? No, said Hans. Did Ruedi want a holiday before he died? No. Did they want to play cards? No. Just to listen to music, in the gloom. Or in the dark. Did the twins want anything at all? They did not.

LAST VANITIES

LAST VANITIES

I

Kurt and Verena Kuster will be celebrating their golden wedding anniversary. The neighbors say how fine it is to celebrate one's golden anniversary. They say it affectionately. "Es est schön." A note of regret almost in their voices. Verena thanks them. After doing nothing all day, Mr. and Mrs. Kuster spent the evenings in their sitting room. Kurt looks grimly at his wife. He had been giving her that grim look for months. Verena wondered what on earth was the matter with her husband. The celebrations were almost upon them now, half a century they had been living together, and now this kind and pleasant-mannered man was looking at her silently, reproachfully. One could sense the reproach in the silent sitting room, it rose from the floor and spread out like a foul-smelling fog, enveloping the plumply impressive furniture. As though from a sandbank, the two of them loomed above these vapors, like evil spirits. "Dirty eyes," Verena thought, watching her husband. "Dirty eyes," Verena goes on thinking, lips barely moving. As tears are dirty too. Grief can warp the eyes. But not in Mr. and Mrs. Kuster's house. Not in Mr. and Mrs. Kuster's marriage. Kurt had never had that look, that torpor, that sloth in the past. Sadness, to Verena's mind, is sloth.

Then they went to bed, each in their separate rooms, giving thanks to God. Yes, they gave thanks, for being able to have separate rooms to pass the night in. She had wanted separate rooms from the start. When he asked her to marry him, she made him promise they would have separate rooms. And now, after fifty years, Kurt says he has premonitions. He has got it into his head that she is ill. He is extremely upset about her being ill. Finally he admitted as much. It was a spring day, not yet noon, the whole day to fill. And, ever thankful to God, at eighty-four Verena has never been so well in all her life. The older she got the better she felt. "I'm not ill at all, Kurt dear," she said. Kurt isn't listening. He'd taken off his jacket, the spring was stifling. An old wool jacket. His shoulders drooped, they didn't look so drooping and frail when he wore a tweed jacket. "Soiled eyes," Verena thought now. Grief smears the eyes. Her husband's hands are small, tapered, his wrists slender, feet tiny. One part of his body—Verena is precise in her observations—has stayed young, adolescent almost. Old age has forgotten to claim it, or them, the small feet her husband kept propped up in bed, bare and white, the toes so finely chiseled they look all of a piece. His legs, so white and feminine, have nothing of the flabby scourge of old age. The years haven't claimed his legs. "I'm afraid," he had told her. And he darted her a disheartened, mean look. Such small, tender, tapered hands ought not to nurse such gloomy thoughts. It was ridiculous that her kind, honest, shy, mild-mannered husband should toy with such morbid ideas. A wife's illness can hardly exhaust the whole world, or destiny, Verena reflected. This was the man she had relied on for fifty years. Amongst other things, she begged him, he mustn't let his slow, measured imagination plunge into the vast universe. And by "vast universe" Verena meant: imagining the death of his fellow men, imagining the death of his wife, plunging into the realm of premonition. "I'm afraid," Kurt repeated.

He wasn't happy that his wife was ill. His gait became uncertain, as if he were afraid of walking. It was Sunday, she saw him coming home with a small pyramid-shaped parcel tied up with a ribbon. Their Sunday tartes aux pommes from Muller's pastry shop. Verena had nudged aside the curtains and watched her husband approach, holding the pyramid shape on the palm of one hand, like a sacred object. Then Kurt rang the bell. He came in slowly, dejected and weary. How long could he go on bringing his wife her Sunday cakes?

But that wasn't the only time Verena spied on her husband. Perhaps it is the destiny of couples to spy on each other. What was it, Verena wondered, that her husband had seen in her to make him fear for her life. What were the outward signs? What on earth could he have seen that she knows nothing of?

They ate in the kitchen, because Kurt liked eating in the kitchen. They sat and waited for their food to cook. Kurt watched the steam from the pans. When he had contemplated that for a while his gaze wandered, forlorn and tainted along tiles and walls. "Weather's stifling," he says. Verena opens the window. Outside, close by, there was another kitchen window, belonging to another apartment. A couple lived there. Like themselves. Same apartment. Same arrangement of rooms, but one less. Same age. The couple in the adjoining apartment slept in the same room in a double bed. She called them "the adjacent couple." They were the continuation of their own rooms. Which then went on in other apartments like their own. They were the continuation of their lives. From her room Verena could hear the couple turning over in bed, the weight of their bodies. Adjacent to their own. The deepening of their sleep. After a struggle with insomnia. They spoke in Berne dialect. They cooked at the same time she cooked. So if Verena opened the window, her steam and food smell went out and theirs came in, their food smell, their steam. It was a kind of communion. Reciprocity. The great substance becoming one. A carniverous exuberance of the one towards the other, one room inside the other. The building was entirely reserved for the old. Old insomniacs. There were five floors. All the apartments had the same layout. Just a few have the extra room. One of those is the apartment of Kurt and Verena Kuster, natives of Canton Uri. And now, while her husband is convinced that she is dying, Verena would like to know where the other couples are from. The couple who sleep in the double bed. Their bathroom has a small frosted-glass window like their own and no one ever visits them. They are going to share the same tombstone. They have been promised the ground, they all have. It's next to the house. House and ground. And dust. The Confederation has arranged things thus. In the best possible way. The cemetery nearby, easy to get to. Their own patch of heather.

Never before has Verena found equality so sinister and dirty—dirty as her husband's eyes are dirty, promiscuous. The equality she had looked forward to in her youth. That she had considered her right—like the separate rooms. If Kurt was imagining her death, now she too can set her face in a look of contrition. She laughed. It all comes from sloth. In the adjacent apartment the couple speak incessantly, chattering in Berne dialect. If their words took up space, the whole building wouldn't be enough to hold them. He is lame, but walks fast. They do the rounds of the apartment. There are trees, flower beds. And the wall. Verena hears them crossing the passageway with swift irregular steps. The steps reach the closet. They go on as far as the sitting room. The sound of the steps stops and the voices begin. It seems they've been talking for centuries. Where are they from? she wonders again. But what does it matter? The building is reserved for Swiss people, retired Swiss workers. It's as if they originally came from the plains of Ukraine, Montenegro, Hungary. Once she read a book about an empire, an army, various races breaking up, and they were just the same, the retired Swiss workers, a dispersed platoon. The cantons blend into lands that stretch away to the steppes.

And right in the middle there was a love story, she had read it when she was young, and all of a sudden she found herself remembering those soldiers, from those scattered populations, those innumerable languages. Now it was as though those soldiers, that mutinous army were living in the old people's building. When she was young the only thing she was interested in was the love story. She skipped distractedly through the pages about the battles and the front. And now those unread pages came back to her as sharply defined as objects of reflection. Sharp as if she had read every word. What did she know of the Ukrainians? What did she know of the world, beyond the border? She had been to Basel once, on their honeymoon. Kurt had taken her as far as Schaffhausen to see the waterfall. And she saw the waterfall and people from all over the world. Perhaps that was the only time she had been close to so many foreigners, when she got out of the rowboat to see the waterfall, high up the rock. And there was a sharp smell. In the middle of nature, the acrid summer smell simmered. Some boys with short pants and grown-up knees had just climbed down from the rock face. Verena was on her honeymoon and paid no attention to the foreigners. She gazed in amazement at the waterfall. And now she forgets the falls but remembers the foreigners with great precision. She remembers what she didn't look at. In the rowboat there was a Japanese man with a Japanese woman. And men talking in a language she had never heard before. They went down to a big hotel. And there were foreigners there too. A group of five or six people speaking another language she didn't know, and she and her husband had waited to one side before going to the reception desk. Respectfully. Foreign languages are a great mystery. She and her husband had been in awe. They hardly dared to go to the reception desk to sign the register. Then they went up to a large room with a big double bed. A landscape with waterfall on the wall. From the window you could see the Rhine. Which she had never seen before and would never see again, except in her imagination. She had seen it again in her imagination. The cradle of our ancestors. In bed she thought how the previous night and nights others had done what they were doing now. The following night it would be them again, not others. They had the room for a week. The first night she felt like an actress, trying to perform what others had done, in the same hotel in the same bed. She was imitating women who went to Basel for their honeymoon. Resolute and romantic, she tried not to think of such things, that way the nuptial ceremony seemed freer from other people's effusions. Each evening Kurt hung their clothes in the wardrobe, on hangers that couldn't be taken out. The clothes they had bought before the wedding. And which would last for so long. The children never came. They were not conceived in the hotel room in Basel overlooking the Rhine, nor on other beds or holidays.

Strange, thinks Verena, that there isn't even one widow or widower in the old people's building. This apartment block for the old was a miraculous place, where all were still united, however lost and dispersed they seemed. Sickly and long lived. And she thought how she, Verena, didn't want to be the first to break the spell. She had the impression that, if someone began to die, it would drag the others after. Death is first and foremost something that contaminates. The law of like following like. If nothing happened in the building, it was because nothing can happen if it hasn't already happened. And since the old people were all still alive, they would only begin to die when someone gave the sign. She repeated her thoughts over and over like a nursery rhyme.

When the building was put up, the Kusters were among the first couples to move in. After which she saw the others come two by two. Then the building is called Eden Haus, as all the homes for the dead, or for those about to die, are called Paradise, Zur Sonne, Aurora. Violent names. The only change she had noticed as the years went by was this: those who had been tall were now less so. The lame man had been tall, when she saw him arrive holding his wife by the elbow. Her husband wasn't so tall now either. She had started to turn up the hem of his pants. Verena knew she wouldn't be shortening them much more now. You can't live long enough to wear down your bones.

When Verena went down to the laundry in the basement, and waited with the other women for the clothes to be tumbled and wrung in the communal machines, everybody watching the water foam in the glass, they were probably wondering for how many more decades they would have to take care of the washing. She had noticed how, imperceptibly, the women had grown smaller too. Their hair fluffy. They gazed at their washing turning in the glass, hands on their knees. She had thought how one fine day their bones would be as clean as fresh laundry. It was convenient having a laundry in the basement. They were self-sufficient.

The couples take meals together, as they do. Verena clears away the dishes, Kurt helps. One may as well do something. She dusts the house with white cotton gloves. She's afraid of dust. She never was when she was younger. Now she's preparing for the essential. She'd often imagined the scene when some policeman or public official found them dead. They look around, marveling to see the flat so clean and tidy. For the old are not always clean, she dreamed of telling the public official who would find her dead. That's why she always kept her and her husband's underwear tidy. And there would be a hint of a smile on her face, in satisfied acknowledgment of the public official's compliments. She couldn't disguise her satisfaction. A word of praise from brutes who so often have to do with homicides can hardly leave her indifferent.

She doesn't want to be the one to lead the way. The lame man has a cough. He's walking even faster. He's always in a hurry, doing nothing. Her destiny, Verena tells herself, is linked to the others', who live exactly as they do. Her husband seems happier now. The doctor has declared her healthy. Mrs. Kuster has nothing wrong with her. No need to worry. Kurt smiled weakly. An illness, Verena had appreciated, would have been an event. It's not up to a doctor to say whether one is healthy or not, Kurt said stubbornly when they got home. But he seemed relieved. For all you might see an illness as a diversion, it's still your wife's illness, and you love your wife. Have to forgo the diversion then. And simply be happy that your wife is in good health. Kurt no longer gives her grim looks. He's not depressed now. And what else can he be, now that he's not depressed? A calm old man, a calm old man as he has been for years. "I feel calm," Kurt says. And he strokes her hand, her still-soft hand, which she withdrew. Verena had become so pensive these last months, she had seen how even depression is a diversion. It seems likely that every married person thinks of the death of their partner. In every affectionate thought there lurks, light as a feather, a murderous thought. It's love, the love that lives on in old couples, that spurs the imagination towards the mental murder of one's partner. A poetic dream. The airiest, most enticing, most delicate of homicides, that spins itself out at the back of the eyes, tenses inside the jack-in-the-box. Where a tune is playing.

II

Verena had understood all this, including her husband's nostalgia for something that had happened, that had come about in his head. In the head of this kindest of men, who hadn't proved fainthearted before such an awful and beguiling dream. It takes courage, Verena thinks, to dream of the infirmities, betrayals, and agonies that inevitably lead to the end. The end of Verena Kuster. In recent months Kurt had fed and frightened himself with the image of his wife's decline. He had cluttered the house with his sadness and bad temper, for he didn't like being left alone. He was within an ace of dreaming that too. Of dreaming of the postmortem. But the doctor has spoilt his after-funeral reverie. Though Kurt hasn't changed his mind about health and how to check up on it.

Kurt sits meekly in the armchair. He has moved it towards the window, which looks out on a wall. And you can see the sky too. He looked at the wall and the sky. He is affectionate now. They even laugh. Mr. and Mrs. Kuster laugh. The adjoining couple hear them laugh. And passing from one wall to the other their laughter takes on a grating metallic sound, as if a farce were being acted out on the other side of the wall. Everything's fine again, they're laughing over trifles. The landscape is intact again, the landscape of their rooms, as if it were new. Verena's blue hair is like her neighbor's, who has less than her, but hides her baldness with curls and clasps.

Kurt opens the window. Wall and sky. The Föhn is blowing again today, the west wind. "There he is, there he is." It's still far away, but he can just make out the bird with the pistachio-colored feathers. "It's him." Kurt greets the bird. He shouldn't be flying to Goschenen or Tiefencastel any more, but back to his relatives in South America. The Föhn is dangerous, sweet and dangerous. It makes people a bit crazy. There are even murders. For nothing. When the west wind blows. The filth of sweetness, that's the Föhn.

The bird seems to be smiling. "Nein, es kann nicht sein," Kurt says out loud. It can't be. Birds can't smile.

Verena was putting pins in a hem. It bothers her when Kurt speaks out loud. For she sews as though in a trance. A hem is an infinity. But now she has to look up. Wings outspread, pistachio, yellow, and purple, a sharp tiny crest on its head. Verena drops her eyes to her sewing. Kurt leans his hands on the sill. The bird is still up in the sky, hovering above the wall as the woman stitches the cloth. It's as if the woman were holding the thread that makes it fly. Now the bird perches its feet on the sill. There's something human about its face, the painted face of women in brothels, Verena thinks, eyes in pools of purple, pink and toasted flesh, the color of whores' blood, Verena thinks. What is wonderful is how this strange, splendid example imprisoned in a sky that is not its own, provokes an instinctive revulsion in her. She can't contain a savage rancor, a rancor partly directed at divine grace. Kurt is so happy. There are happy birds that escape from their native skies, perhaps upon feeling the west wind blow, this wind that makes men a bit crazy, and other creatures too. Verena wasn't pleased by the neighbors' eager congratulations on her golden wedding anniversary. No, congratulations are not for the likes of her. After her husband had dreamed she was ill and then got drunk on the idea. Thank heaven—and if she'd said it once she'd said it a thousand times—darning was a great consolation. She had even started darning old tablecloths. She darned so well, and meantime she thought that life too had been one long darning. Everything wears out, she thought, even her happy marriage, in the paradise of this home for the aged. Invisible stitches leave no trace on the fabric, like the breath of an angel.

Verena felt young and peaceful. The only thing that interested her was her old age, she had grown vain. She never had been in the past. She'd been modest when she was young. And she'd seen the other old folk swelling with vanity too. At this time of life, stubborn, reluctant to die, one feels vain. Of this she's quite sure: vanity is not for the young. It's not for beautiful women and handsome boys. No, theirs is just a by-product of vanity. She had watched them, the young, when she went out, compared them with herself. She's decrepit, those youngsters would say. Now she kept herself neat and tidy, not just because of that silly business of the police finding her dead and saying: "But how clean her house is." That was an excuse. An excuse for the police. Only God knew how vain she really was. It's something that goes beyond the physical, something very deep, terribly deep. Not even desperation could be so deep. But then thinking about it Verena has a start. Perhaps the vanity of the old is desperation. Her puffy hair goes from blue to ash, her blue eyes to ash and yellow, eyes watching her husband with defiance and a celestial supremacy.

The Föhn is blowing again today. Kurt has taken off his jacket. How irritating the weather is, when the wind is from the west. The flowers wilt in the untimely heat, unfulfilled colors in their petals. Kurt talks to himself. Verena sews. Six hours to Vespers. Kurt leans his hands on the windowsill. The bird seems to be dancing, tracing out an ellipse. Kurt has already thrown one leg over the sill, and now he lifts the other over too. His body is lighter than a thought. Now he's lying at the bottom. Slowly and calmly, Verena sets aside her sewing. Like her, all the tenants are looking out the window. And it's strange, thinks Verena, it's as if they had tiaras on their heads. She hangs up her husband's jacket. She doesn't want any mess. She puts the armchair back where it belongs. And is ready to accept condolences.

III

The tenants are dressed in Sunday best and mourning. They like to look smart. Then they know that at an occasion like a funeral everybody will be watching everybody else and making comparisons. Seeing how far gone they all are. After ten minutes' rather hurried walking they enter the public gardens. The clods are waiting. Verena and the old folks are getting impatient.

Verena stands a little to one side. People shake her hand. They're sorry they didn't make it to their golden wedding. "Es tut uns leid." There is no emotion in their voices. For the first few days Verena behaves as if her husband were at home. All she has to do is show her regret. After a few weeks she acts as though an audience were watching. She bends defiantly over her sewing, as if she had a dagger in her hand. The audience don't have needles to wield, but sit in front of her, as though in court. It's the courtroom Verena has always dreamed of. And she is the accused. Verena the murderer. She's wearing a simple dress that falls to her ankles. Her shoes are black. Not a single jewel. She has never had any jewels. Only her gold ring. She lifts her hand, to show she has nothing but her gold ring. And her marriage.

Only now, now that she's old, does she feel she must tell the truth. It's when you're old, she thought, that it's essential to tell the truth, the truth about intentions. Verena must present her thoughts. The way a traveling salesman shows his wares. Verena touches her head. How intelligent that old thing is, covered with its soft blue hair, and how smooth and bright her forehead is after years of dullness. Now that he has fallen from the window. Everything becomes so clear after a death, so sharp. Thoughts flare up, like flames from her kitchen gas-ring. And she wants to show how a simple woman, an old woman. . . . (Though the words, old and simple, are so ridiculous and stupid: an old person is never simple, and least of all herself. They're not the right words for her.)

Verena Kuster helped her husband to throw himself down from the window. She senses a certain amazement in the courtroom. Amazement that, only a few days before her golden wedding anniversary, this insignificant woman could have punished her husband with death. Her story is grabbing the public's attention. She has told the judge how her husband made up that business of her being ill. She tells him about her husband, how depressed and irritable he was when he thought she was done for. And how crestfallen when he found out she wasn't ill at all.

That's what she couldn't forgive him. Kurt, says Verena, in her cold, reasonable voice, was upset about her being healthy. He was disappointed. Disappointed with destiny. Could she go on living with a man who was upset that she wasn't dead? That's what she would put to the court. That's what Verena put to herself as she sewed. The day it happened her husband went on and on like a lunatic saying how that strange creature flying about was calling to him, how that person flying about (because it was a person now), this flying thing, had flown off its celestial course. No one saw her. There are no witnesses. It's she herself, with her excessive respect for the truth, who tells the court what she meant to do. Verena is meticulous, and in the same way she sews her fabrics, so now she sews together words and thoughts. The murder was her prettiest embroidery ever. She heard applause. How many women would kill their husbands like that, without being murderers. In the end she has helped him to achieve his dream. Made his dream come true. Kurt wanted to fly. And to fly, says Verena brusquely to the court, you have to fall. In the street a stranger doffed his hat as she passed. The people of Tiefencastel are polite to those who have lost a loved one. Children run after her, wanting to see the face of the woman who says she helped her husband fall out the window. All her life she had saved her silk nightdresses, the ones she bought before the wedding. Now she uses them all the time. And perhaps they suit her bony figure better than in the past. She felt sure of the way she held herself now, enjoyed a certain sensual pleasure in feeling the silk caress her bones. I'm wearing this nightdress, she thought, für mich selbst. For myself. Her whole old age was for herself. She had finally entered into her body. And, topping her body, her small, fluffy head. Her eyes, two night-lights. A totem. To enter into the totem, that is real vanity. She didn't need mirrors now. A totem doesn't look in the mirror. It is driven into the earth. Its hair flutters in the wind, the west wind. Mrs. Kuster presses her index finger on the round box of her rouge, spreads it on her cheeks. On her mouth. She's prettier now than in the past.

They didn't find her guilty, not even of neglecting to come to her husband's aid. They merely offended her, by mistaking her words for blather, the blather of an old belle. And vanity, in so democratic a country, is punished. Even the appropriation of a crime you didn't commit is a punishable offence. Thus Verena's thoughts, shortly before falling asleep. To push one's husband out of the window, using no more than words, persuasion, is a form of spirituality. She confessed that—and even confessing a wicked thought, a murderous thought, of which there is no earthly proof, is spirituality. . . . She has come closer to the sky, she has been slighted by men who wouldn't believe she was telling the truth.

Verena is happy. Now she too stares at the sky, as her husband did before her. One day perhaps, to be even nearer the sky, she too will throw herself down. On the other hand, thinks Verena, throwing yourself out of the window is a sin. And she would prefer a quiet atonement. Such is her way.